For baby Isak— who hardly ever wears pants

First edition 2017

Library of Congress Catalog Card Number pending
ISBN 978-0-7636-8984-1

17 18 19 20 21 22 TLF 10 9 8 7 6 5 4 3 2 1

Printed in Dongguan, Guangdong, China

This book was typeset in Kosmik.
The illustrations were created digitally.

Candlewick Press
99 Dover Street
Somerville, Massachusetts 02144

visit us at www.candlewick.com

Giant Pants

MARK FEARING

CANDLEWICK PRESS

Belbum was a giant.

And like most giants, he was good at stomping, napping, and losing things.

One morning, he lost something very important . . .

HIS PANTS.

Belbum had only one pair of pants, which the tailor in town had made just for him. And now they were lost.

He searched his whole house.

NO PANTS.

After peeking outside to make sure no one was watching, he searched his backyard.

NO PANTS.

Giants are also good at being angry.

And now Belbum was

ANGRY.

Unfortunately, that didn't help him find his pants.

But it did make a big mess.

Then he had a thought: maybe his friends could help!

He checked that no one was around to see him,
and then he headed off into the woods.

First he went to see his friend Polyphemus, the cyclops.

"I've lost my pants," Belbum explained. "Can I borrow a
pair of yours?"

"I only wear togas," Polyphemus said. "But I have an extra one."

"Of course I did!"

Belbum roared, and marched away.

He went straight to see Old Grint,
who was a very wise gnome.

"I've lost my pants," Belbum said.

"I can see that," said Old Grint.

"You can try a pair of mine — they're stretchy!"

Belbum **tried** to try them on.

"Not stretchy enough!"
he bellowed.

Belbum **tried** to try them on.

"Not stretchy enough!" he bellowed.

"Did you search your room?"
Old Grint asked.

"YES!" Belbum yelled
as he stomped off.

He found Lucy, the unicorn, and told her that he'd lost his pants.
"I don't wear pants. You could try that!" she suggested.

"I HAVE TRIED IT, AND I DON'T LIKE IT!"

"Have you checked your dresser?" Lucy called,
but Belbum had already stormed off.

He needed pants — giant pants —
and there was only one way to get them.

He had to walk to the tailor in town—

WITH NO PANTS.

When he got there, the tailor made
him a new pair of giant pants.

Belbum even decided to get
a few extra pairs.

On his way back,
he gave each of his
friends a pair of
giant pants.

(Just in case he
ever lost his again.)

When he got home, he cleaned up the mess he'd made and put away his new pants . . .

and that's when he found

his old pants.